That's Not All I Want for Christmas

written by Lynn Hodges and Sue Buchanan

illustrated by Meredith Johnson

FaithKidz®
Equipping Kids for Life

An Imprint of Cook Communications Ministries
Colorado Springs, CO

Faith Parenting Guide
Ages 4-7
Selflessness

A Faith Parenting Guide
can be found starting on page 33

Faith Kidz® is an imprint of Cook Communications Ministries
Colorado Springs, Colorado 80918
Cook Communications, Paris, Ontario
Kingsway Communications, Eastbourne, England

THAT'S NOT ALL I WANT FOR CHRISTMAS ©2004 by Lynn Hodges and Sue Buchanan
Illustrated by Meredith Johnson

First printing, 2004
Printed in India
1 2 3 4 5 6 7 8 9 10 Printing/Year 08 07 06 05 04

ISBN: 0781440785

Editors: Heather Gemmen and Mary McNeil
Creative Director: Randy Maid
Design Manager: Nancy L. Haskins
Designer: Helen H. Harrison

Dedication

To my parents, Harry and Inez Unger,
who have mastered the art of giving of themselves...always available.
Thank you for your selflessness. I love you.
Lynn

All I want for Christmas is my family... and the gifts they bring!
Besides the well-chosen tangibles that come wrapped in glittery
paper and silky ribbon, there are the more important intangibles.
Love!   Joy!   Caring!   Enthusiasm!   Selflessness!   Craziness!
And serendipity!
Wayne, Mindy, Dana, Barry, Cara, Kirby,
Jon and Becky — this book's for you!
SB

All I want for Christmas this year is for all the poor hungry children in the world to have lots of food ... and warm clothes."

Ashton scratched her forehead with her pencil.

4

Hmm ... That's not all I want for Christmas. All I want for Christmas this year is for the poor hungry children in the world to have lots of food ... and warm clothes ... and maybe a few toys ... and ... for me ..." she wrote, "... a makeup kit with twenty-seven colors of eye shadow and fourteen lipsticks. A makeup kit that looks like a little suitcase and has a mirror in the top. That's it. The perfect Christmas."

She put down her pencil, but it seemed to jump right back into her hands.
"Hmm ... That's not all I want for Christmas." She began to scribble again.

All I want for Christmas this year is for the poor hungry children in the world to have lots of food and warm clothes and toys, and a makeup kit for me … and the white bunny-fur jacket I tried on at the mall … and … the ring and ear-rings with the huge genuine imitation rubies … and … a new kitty … and …"
Ashton twirled a lock of her hair with her finger and stared at her list.

Ashton Danbury had written down everything she could possibly imagine on her Christmas list, and she knew she would get all that and more. She always did. She had no brothers or sisters, and her parents worked long hours to make sure Ashton had it all.

I can't wait for Christmas! It's my favorite day of the year. I'll get everything I want, and everyone will want to play with me. Everyone will want to *be* me!"

Christmas morning came, and as always, boxes were stacked as high as the sparkling tree. Ashton tore paper and pulled ribbon until toys, clothes, and anything else a girl could want covered the floor. She hardly even looked at one present before opening another. With several packages still waiting to be unwrapped, Ashton yawned and announced, "I'm tired of doing this; I think I'll watch TV!"

11

The next day, the doorbell rang, and Ashton ran to see who was there.

Mr. Grant, the yardman, had come to shovel the driveway, and Debbie, his granddaughter, had tagged along.

Oh, hello, Debbie."

"Hi, Ashton."

"I'm sure you want to see what I got for Christmas, right?"

"Um, I'd love to," said Debbie, and she followed Ashton up the stairs.

13

Ashton's room glittered and shone with stacks of newly opened presents. Debbie went straight to the bright silver makeup kit, gingerly raised the lid, and tilted the mirror.

Don't touch that!" huffed Ashton, and she snapped the lid shut. "I want to use it first."

15

"Sorry," Debbie said as she picked up the new bunny-fur coat from the floor and buried her nose in its softness.

"Stop!" Ashton screeched. "You'll get it dirty!"

"Sorry," said Debbie.

Debbie turned and spotted a doll that looked just like Ashton. Her eyes lit up, but before she could even reach out for it, Ashton stepped in front of her.

"Don't even think about it!" she said with her hand on her hip. "It's very expensive."

"Sorry," said Debbie.

Debbie cautiously admired some new jewelry. This time she clasped her hands behind her back.

"What are you doing?" Ashton asked as she grabbed the jewelry. "I haven't even tried it on yet. So what did you get?"

18

W ell," Debbie said warmly, "my mom made this scarf for me. Her hands are really stiff and sore, so it took her a long time." Debbie rubbed the fuzzy scarf against her cheek and then reached into her pocket. "My grandma made these mittens to match. And my dad gave me this golden key chain that belonged to him when he was a kid."

19

J ust three presents? That's it?"

"My mom says that's how many presents Jesus got, so why should we get more than he did?"

Ashton rolled her eyes and muttered, "Mittens? For Christmas? How boring!"

Debbie shrugged. "Hey, let's go outside and build a giant snowman."

21

Ashton laughed. "Why should I play outside when I have all this fun stuff in here?"

Okay, well, see you later, then." Debbie scampered out the door.

Before long kids from nearby homes filled Ashton's front yard, laughing and yelling. She watched as they threw snowballs and struggled to put together the giant snowman.

Just then, Debbie stuck her head in the door and said, "Are you sure you don't want to play?"

"I don't have anything to play in." Ashton's eyes filled with tears. "I'm not allowed to get my clothes dirty," she said, turning away from the door.

"Wait! You can wear my brother's jacket and boots. They're in the truck. He won't care if they get dirty! And I'll let you borrow one of my mittens!"

25

In a borrowed jacket and boots that were four sizes too big, Ashton clomped around her yard, making snow angels and snow forts with the kids. She even clipped one of the boys with a snowball. And he got her back—right in the neck!

"You're the abobimal snowman!" he shouted as he fell to the ground, pretending to be injured.

"Abonibal ... abominal ... abom— you are!" Ashton flashed a victory smile.

Ashton whispered to Debbie, "Wait here," and ran into the house.

27

Debbie was putting the finishing touches on the snowman when Ashton tapped her on the shoulder and held out her mittened hand. Together, the two of them reached as high as they could to place the genuine imitation ruby buttons on their frosty friend.

That night, Ashton carefully laid out her favorite Christmas gifts on her bedroom floor.

Before she went to sleep she thought about her new friend and about how close she had come to missing the very best day of her life.

"Dear God," she prayed, "I was pretty abom … abominal … abominable today." Just thinking the word made her giggle.

"Oh, no! I didn't even think about Jesus on his birthday. Thank you, God, for sending him and for loving me so much. Thank you for Debbie, and please bless all the poor hungry children in the world who need food and warm clothes."

First thing next morning Ashton picked up the phone. "Debbie, I'm sorry I acted like the abob ... abom ... that snowman!" They both giggled. "Could you maybe come over and play? Spend the day? We'll drink cocoa and build a snow lady next to our snowman ... and ... play dolls ... and ... dress up ... and ... Debbie! Guess what? I have a present for you. An after-Christmas present." Ashton's voice became quiet. "Matter of fact, I have three!"

That's Not All I Want for Christmas

Life Issue: I want my children to enjoy celebrating Jesus at Christmas.
Spiritual Building Block: **Selflessness**

Use the following activities to help your children value the gift of Jesus Christ.

Sight:
Play a light-spotting game with your child. As you drive around during the Christmas season, look for decorative lights in windows and on rooftops. See who can be the first to call out "lights!"

Whoever calls it first gets to name something unselfish that he or she has seen someone do recently. If your neighborhood has too many lights to make this practical, choose just one kind of Christmas light, such as windowsill candles that can be seen from the street.

Talk together about how recognizing loving actions in others is something Jesus did. Encourage your child to "light up" someone's life by doing something unselfish or special for another. Talk about how God was unselfish by giving his Son for us.

That's Not All I Want for Christmas

Life Issue: **I want my children to enjoy celebrating Jesus at Christmas.**
Spiritual Building Block: **Selflessness**

Use the following activities to help your children value the gift of Jesus Christ.

Sound:

Help your child make a game of listening for and saying unselfish things. First talk about sentences kids say that show caring or unselfishness. You could suggest these four:

Would you like to play with me?

What would you like to do next?

Why don't you go in front of me?

I like the way you _____ (fill in the blank with an honest answer).

Then use these sentences in a game. Together with your child, choose one sentence to focus on each day or during each playtime with another child. Encourage your child to use the chosen sentence. Some kids will like to keep count. Ask your child to listen for when a friend says something similar. Also share together about how listening to friends' feelings and caring about them makes us more like Jesus.

That's Not All I Want for Christmas

Life Issue: I want my children to enjoy celebrating Jesus at Christmas.
Spiritual Building Block: **Selflessness**

Use the following activities to help your children value the gift of Jesus Christ.

Touch:

Help your child make or purchase a small Christmas gift. Wrap it up for an underprivileged child or family. Check with your church or a Christian charity to help you find someone who needs a gift this Christmas. Let your child do as much of the "hands-on" work as possible. As you create, shop, and wrap together, talk about how Jesus cared about the poor and gave of himself to show his love for them.

The Word at Work Around the World

What would you do if you wanted to share God's love with children on the streets of your city? That's the dilemma David C. Cook faced in 1870's Chicago. His answer was to create literature that would capture children's hearts.

Out of those humble beginnings grew a worldwide ministry that has used literature to proclaim God's love and disciple generation after generation. Cook Communications Ministries is committed to personal discipleship—to helping people of all ages learn God's Word, embrace his salvation, walk in his ways, and minister in his name.

Faith Kidz, RiverOak, Honor, Life Journey, Victor, NextGen . . . every time you purchase a book produced by Cook Communications Ministries, you not only meet a vital personal need in your life or in the life of someone you love, but you're also a part of ministering to José in Colombia, Humberto in Chile, Gousa in India, or Lidiane in Brazil. You help make it possible for a pastor in China, a child in Peru, or a mother in West Africa to enjoy a life-changing book. And because you helped, children and adults around the world are learning God's Word and walking in his ways.

Thank you for your partnership in helping to disciple the world. May God bless you with the power of his Word in your life.

For more information about our international ministries,
visit www.ccmi.org.